The Popcorn Astronauts

And Other Biteable Rhymes

Deborah Ruddell

illustrated by

Joan Rankin

Margaret K. McElderry Books
New York London Toronto Sydney New Delhi

MARGARET K. McELDERRY BOOKS

An imprint of Simon & Schuster Children's Publishing Division

1230 Avenue of the Americas, New York, New York 10020

Text copyright © 2015 by Deborah Ruddell

Illustrations copyright © 2015 by Joan Rankin

MARGARET K. McELDERRY BOOKS is a trademark of Simon & Schuster, Inc.

For information about special discounts for bulk purchases, please contact Simon & Schuster Special Sales at 1-866-506-1949 or business@simonandschuster.com.

The Simon & Schuster Speakers Bureau can bring authors to your live event. For more information or to book an event, contact the Simon & Schuster Speakers Bureau at 1-866-248-3049 or visit our website at www.simonspeakers.com.

Book design by Debra Sfetsios-Conover

The text for this book is set in Frolic JF.

The illustrations for this book are rendered in watercolor.

Manufactured in China

0115 SCP

10 9 8 7 6 5 4 3 2 1

Library of Congress Cataloging-in-Publication Data

Ruddell, Deborah.

[Poems. Selections]

The popcorn astronauts : and other biteable rhymes / Deborah Ruddell ; illustrated by Joan Rankin.—First Edition.

pages cm

Audience: Grade: K to Grade 3.

Audience: Age: 4-8.

ISBN 978-1-4424-6555-8 (Hardcover)—ISBN 978-1-4424-6556-5 (eBook)

I. Rankin, Joan, ill. II. Title.

PS3618.U337A6 2015

811'.6—dc23

2013037332

To Jessy and Ben,
my long-ago brownie assistants,
with love
—D. R.

To Deborah Ruddell for her
delightful poems
that have been such fun
to illustrate
—J. R.

The Strawberry Queen

You'll know her the minute she enters the room
by the first little whiff of her springtime perfume
and her elegant suit—which is *beaded* and red—
and the leafy, green crown on the top of her head.

Remember to bow and address her as *Ma'am*,
but don't say a *word* about strawberry jam.

Lickety-Split Picnic

Put a shade tree in the basket

with a baseball and a blanket

and the green grapes and the baked beans

and your bow-wow and your blue jeans

and a hot dog and a hilltop

and the cupcakes and the flip-flops

and a daydream and a drumstick . . .

easy-breezy, it's a PICNIC!

A Smoothie Supreme

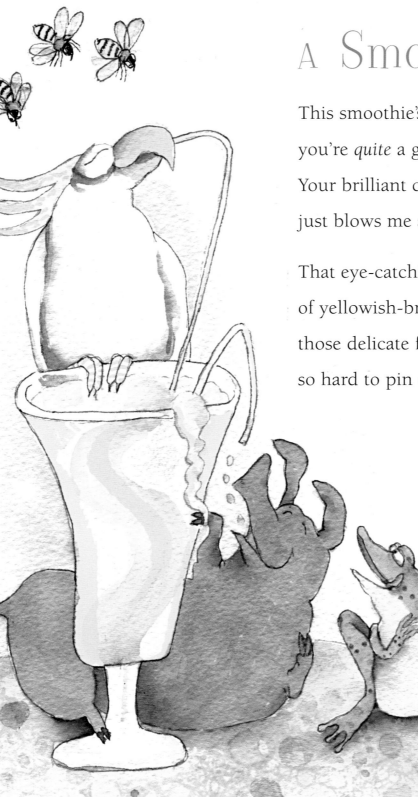

This smoothie's a doozie—
you're *quite* a gourmet!
Your brilliant concoction
just blows me away!

That eye-catching color
of yellowish-brown,
those delicate flavors,
so hard to pin down . . .

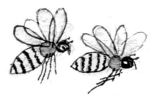

A whisper of pickle
is what I detect,
with glimmers of turnip
I didn't expect!

A dusty old beehive?
A handful of hail?
Unless I'm mistaken,
the slime from a snail.

The mudpuddle splashes
are really delish,
and the finishing touch
is that nubbin of fish!

The Big Question

I'm wondering if you would mind

or would you ever be inclined

or is there any outside chance

(because I'm asking in advance)

that you could maybe find a way,

that it would somehow be okay . . .

Well, here's the thing I need to know . . .

I hate to ask, but here I go:

Soooo . . . do you think that you could share

that yummy-looking lemon square?

Only Guacamole!

Even though it's lumpy and it's avocado green,
like the porridge for an ogre or a troll,
nothing on the table makes my eyes light up
like a little guacamole in a bowl!

Only guacamole has that guacamole taste—
to explain it, I could write a dozen books!
That would take forever, so I'll just say this:
guacamole's *so* much better than it looks!

Welcome to Watermelon Lake!

It's icy cold, so our advice
is take a breath and don't think twice.
Just jump right in—you'll never sink—
and did we mention that it's PINK?

That's right, it's PINK! And what is more,
you're sure to like the pale green shore,
and how you feel so *fresh* and *new*—
you'll love it here, we promise you!

But wait, there's more! This place is *sweet*!
We even have a little fleet
of small black boats for summer fun—
enough of them for everyone!

The Picky Ogre

Bob is an ogre,

the kind of an ogre

who only eats corn on the cob.

Offer him lobster

or blueberry cobbler,

and Bob will most probably sob.

For Bob is an ogre,

the kind of an ogre

who *only* eats corn on the cob.

Recipe for Raisins

One Serving

You take a bunch of juicy grapes
and dry them in the sun.
You shrink them down to half their size,
and you may *think* they're done.

But let them go until they look
like wrinkled rubber rocks
and have the bold, enchanting taste
of well-worn pirate socks.

And there you are! They're *perfect* now,
exactly as you planned,
with all the bug-like chewiness
that raisin fans demand.

Speaking of Peaches . . .

There is *so* much to say about peaches,
but it's hard to know where to begin.
Do you start with the flowery fragrance,
or the summery sweetness within?

Or the juice, as it stickily trickles
from your lips to the tip of your chin?
Or the sunset of beautiful colors
on the flannelpajamaty skin?

How a Poet Orders a Shake

"A frosty cup of moonlight, please,"

the poet murmurs, low.

"As mushy as a mittenful

of slightly melted snow . . .

And *softer* than a summer cloud

and *paler* than a swan

and *pearlier* than polar bears,"

the poet rambles on . . .

"And let it be at least as sweet

as icing on a cake.

In other words,

my usual:

a small vanilla shake."

Voyage of the Great Baked Potato Canoes

"Away, away, to Green Bean Bay!"

said the Great Baked Potato Canoes.

They left the dock at six o'clock

for the dangerous dinner-plate cruise.

They oozed with steam and sour cream.

They were loaded with bacon and chives.

But *silverware* was *everywhere*—

and they barely escaped with their lives.

Your Choices at the Totally Toast Café

White Bread or Wheat Bread

or Blueberry Swirl

Pumpkin-Banana

or Raspberry Twirl

One or Two Slices

Raisins, or No

Straight or Diagonal

Here or To-Go

Perfectly Golden

or Medium Rare

Honey or Cinnamon

Buttered or Bare

Marmalade flavors:

Papaya or Prune

Orange or Cherry . . .

More Coming Soon!

21 Things to Do with an Apple

Wash it

Dry it

Apple-pie it

Bite it

Gnaw it

Paint it

Draw it

Twirl it

Float it

Caramel-coat it

Lunch it

Crunch it

Sunday-brunch it

Peel it

Slice it

Cinnamon-spice it

Sell it

Spell it

Show-and-tell it

Tug-of-war it

Just ignore it

Menu for a Gray Day

A cantaloupe for breakfast
with a slice of tangerine,
an apricot for dinner
and a carrot in between.

A nibble of a mango
when you feel the time is right,
and . . .
a bite of orange sherbet
in the middle of the night.

The Last Brownie

The brownie's in the kitchen.
On the counter. All alone.
As hard and square and rugged
as a brownie made of stone.

But who will have the courage
to bite its rocky crust?
To grind it with their molars
into bits of brownie dust?

It's true, the brownie boulder
will be difficult to chew.
But someone has to do it,
and the hero could be you.

Dracula's Late-Night Bite

Count Dracula rises and opens his eyes.
For a moment, he stares into space.
He straightens his sash and he sprinkles a splash
of cologne on his pillowy face.

Yes, night after night, he goes out for a bite,
but it's always the same old routine:
He slicks back his bangs and he flosses his fangs
and he dines on the same old cuisine.

"It's time for a change! Something daring and strange!"
shouts the count, with his fist in the air.
He orders a pizza and gloomily eats
all alone in his creaky old chair.

"What marvelous fun," sighs the count when he's done,
as he brushes the crumbs from his shirt.
Then . . .
He slicks back his bangs and he flosses his fangs
and he glides out the door for dessert.

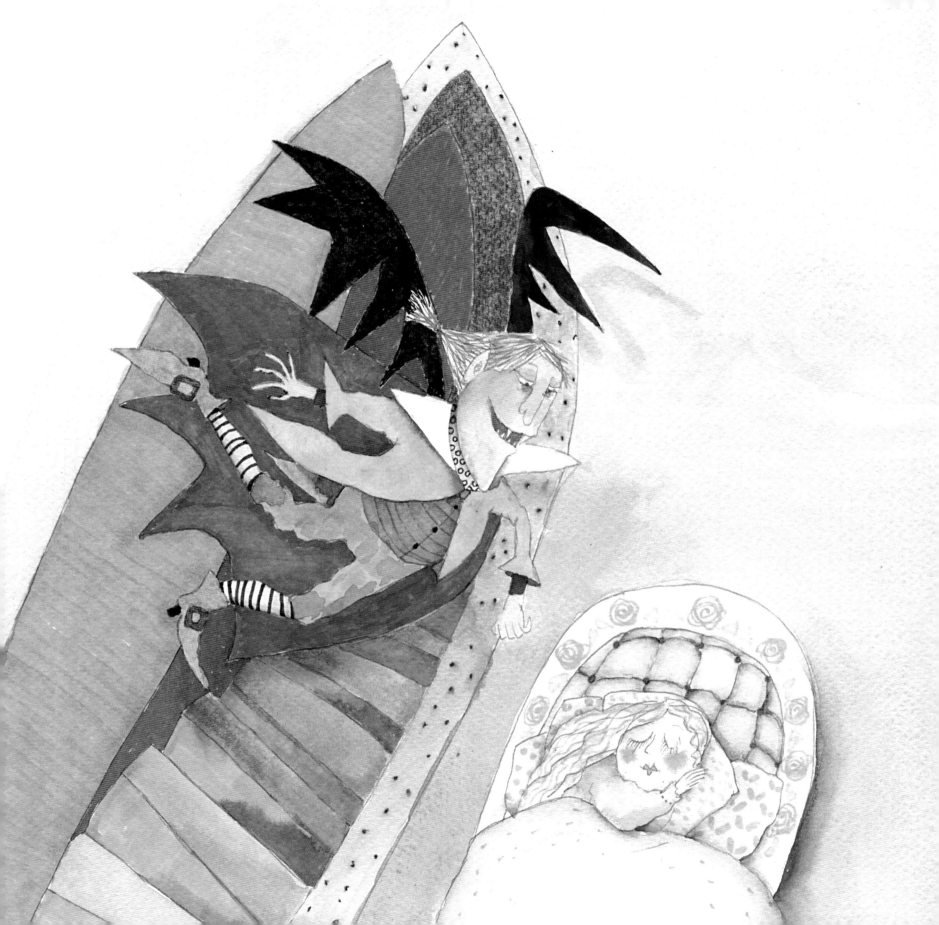

Arrival of the Popcorn Astronauts

The daring popcorn astronauts
are brave beyond compare—
they scramble into puffy suits
and hurtle through the air.

And when they land, we say *hooray*
and crowd around the spot
to salt the little astronauts
and eat them while they're hot.

Stand and Cheer for
MAC and CHEESE!

The Superstars of Suppertime!

The Tip-Top Team! The Perfect Pair!

The Dazzlers of the Dinner Plate!

The Lunchroom Legends, *Everywhere*!

The Noodles Nibbled Nationwide!

The Famous Food Celebrities!

The Couple that You Know and Love!

The One, the Only,

MAC and CHEESE!

Gingerbread House Makeover

Remove the slabs of gingerbread
and every candy cane!
Away with all gumdrop shrubs—
let *none* of them remain!

And picture now a *healthy* house,
admired from coast to coast,
adorned with corn and carrot sticks
and built of whole wheat toast . . .

The radish roses near the walk,
the grove of broccoli trees,
the teeny-weeny doorknobs made
of bright green peas . . .

The chimney built of garlic cloves
and pinto-bean cement,
the cauliflower stepping stones,
the fresh, inviting scent!

The Cocoa Cabana

On an ice-skating pond in the state of Montana,
there's a little red tent called the Cocoa Cabana.

Calling all skaters, the big and the small!
Marshmallow-Peppermint Cocoa for all!

The chef is a girl in a purple bandana,
who goes by the name of Diana-Suzanna.

Calling all skaters, the big and the small!
Marshmallow-Peppermint Cocoa for all!

The cocoa is famous from here to Havana,
so, skaters, let's go to the Cocoa Cabana!

Calling all skaters, the big and the small!
Marshmallow-Peppermint Cocoa for all!

The World's Biggest Birthday Cake

The cake was a whopper, and I've heard it said,

the sprinkles *alone* were the size of your head.

The chocolate frosting was twenty feet deep,

and the climb up the sides was ferociously steep.

But up on the top there was *so* much to see.

A candle, I'm told, was as tall as a tree!

Spectacular roses as high as your shoulders

and fabulous flavors of jellybean boulders!

The lollipop forest was sparkled with snow.

The singing rang out to the valley below.

The sky, so they say, was impossibly blue,

and everyone's craziest wishes came true.